EVERYONE LOVES
POLLY DIAMOND AND THE MAGIC BOOK:

Polly Diamond

and the Super Stunning Spectacular School Fair

BOOK 2

Alice Kuipers

chronicle books · san francisco

Diana Toledano

Library of Congress Cataloging-in-Publication Data:
Names: Kuipers, Alice, 1979- author. | Toledano, Diana, illustrator.
Title: Polly Diamond and the super stunning spectacular school fair
/ Alice Kuipers ; Diana Toledano [illustrator].
Description: San Francisco : Chronicle Books, [2019] | Summary: Today is the school book fair,
which is very exciting for Polly Diamond, who loves books and writing,
and who possesses a magic book which turns anything she writes into reality—
but she also has to be careful because sometimes her book,
Spell, does not quite understand a word and misinterpretations can be catastrophic.
Identifiers: LCCN 2018009423 | ISBN 9781452152332 (alk. paper)
Subjects: LCSH: Magic–Juvenile fiction. | Books and reading–Juvenile fiction. | Fairs–Juvenile fiction.
| Schools–Juvenile fiction. | Humorous stories. | CYAC: Magic–Fiction. | Books and reading–Fiction. |
Fairs–Fiction. | Schools–Fiction. | Humorous stories. | LCGFT: Humorous fiction.
Classification: LCC PZ7.K9490146 Pr 2019 | DDC 823.92 [Fic] —dc23 LC record available at
https://lccn.loc.gov/2018009423

Manufactured in China.

Design by Sara Gillingham Studio.
Typeset in Chapparal and Crayon Nouveau.

10 9 8 7 6 5 4 3 2 1

Chronicle Books LLC, 680 Second Street, San Francisco, California 94107

Chronicle Books—we see things differently. Become part of our community
at www.chroniclekids.com.

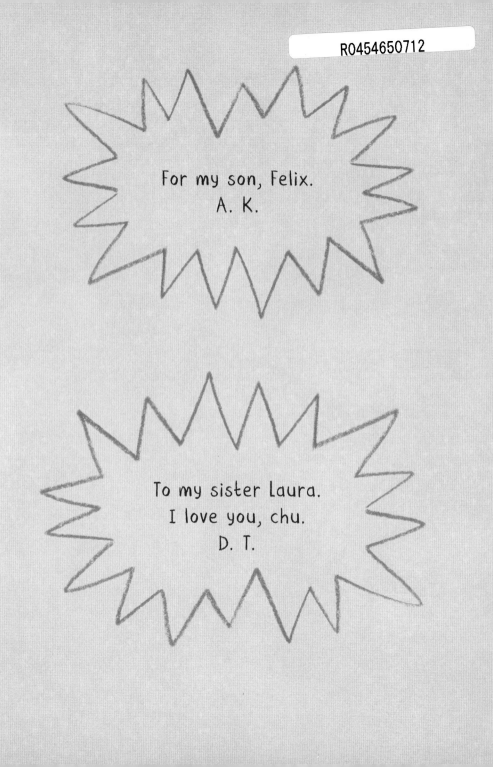

ONE

Three Reasons Today Will Be Spectacular

1. *Spectacular* is my Word of the Day. My dad got me a word calendar so I'd remember the date. Instead, I remember the new words. I love words. Especially words like *spectacular* because it has four syllables. My name, **Polly Diamond**, also has four syllables. My teacher, Ms. Hairball, told us that a syllable is a beat in a word. She beat her hands on her knees. Pol-ly Dia-mond.

2. *Spectacular* means a large, fantastic display. Which is an extra-good word for School Fair Day— which is today! The school fair is all about books. And I love books.

3. Also, I have a super-spectacular book. A *magic* book. Everything I write in my book comes true. I know! Spectacular!

My magic book is sitting next to my breakfast muffin. It—my book, not my muffin—has a turquoise cover. Turquoise is my favorite color. My glasses are turquoise, my sneakers are turquoise, my T-shirt has turquoise triangles. *Turquoise* is a hard word to spell. But I am an excellent speller. I can spell *turquoise*! I love spelling so much that I named my magic book Spell. Spell means THREE things!

1. A moment in time.
2. To spell a word.
3. And a *magic* spell.

Perfect! Because Spell IS magic!

I turn to a blank page in my magic book. I write:

Hi, Spell! Today is going be SPECTACULAR!

A tiny black dot pops onto the page. My book is writing back to me!

Spectacular?

I write: It's School Fair Day.

Does everyone have to play fair on School Fair Day?

No! Silly! *Fair* also means an exhibition! A celebration! A party! And I want to make it spectacular—with you!

My little sister, Anna, runs into the kitchen and jumps on Dad. "ARRGH," he groans dramatically. He wrestles Anna into his arms.

"Daddy, stop!" Anna shrieks. "My wings!"

She wriggles free and straightens her fairy wings. "I'm a fairy today, Polly," she tells me. She snatches my muffin.

I stick my tongue out at her and take a new muffin from the tin. I eat it quickly. If I wrote *Anna is a muffin* in Spell, then, *POP!*, Anna would turn into a muffin! Maybe later.

Anna reaches a sticky hand for Spell.

"Don't touch my book," I say. I turn back to Spell and write: I don't have any ideas for the school fair. But I will soon. Ideas are my specialty.

Fantastic.

Fun. Fantabulous. I love it when words all start with the same letter. Ms. Hairball says this is called alliteration. I call it *fabuloso*!

I don't think *fantabulous* is a word.

I take my old, tattered dictionary down from the top bookshelf. My granny gave it to me. I love the smell of the pages. I love all the words. I go to the letter **F**. I look for *fantabulous.* It is not there. Upstairs, I hear our new baby brother, Finn, yelling. His name is Finn Basil Diamond. I love his middle name—it is a boy's name AND it is the name of an herb. Finn yells again. He is a very yelly baby. *Yelly* is not a real word. But it should be. It describes baby Finn perfectly. I look for the word *yelly* in my dictionary. It is also not there.

I have invented TWO new words! I imagine a dictionary with the words *fantabulous* and *yelly* in it. Under both words would be written: *Invented by Polly Diamond.*

Dad taps my arm. He pops my imagination bubble. "Tick-tock, look at the clock."

Time for school! I pick up Spell and run out of the kitchen. I put on my turquoise rubber boots and grab my raincoat. It has huge pockets. I put Spell in one pocket. Then I shout goodbye to my family.

Dad calls out, "Did you remember your backpack?"

Whoops. I grab it.

I run to the door. Then turn back. *Double-whoops.* I put my shiny new dictionary in my backpack. We are donating a book today, but I can't donate my old dictionary! I love it too much!

"See you at the Super Stunning Spectacular School Fair," I call as I run out the door.

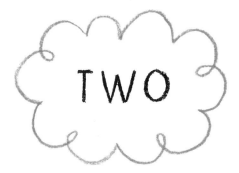

TWO

Outside I wade into the biggest puddle I see.
I imagine I'm exploring a huge lake. I imagine a
monster at the bottom. I get to the other side of
the puddle. I pull out Spell. I lean on my knee and
wibble-wobble write:

A Story About the Puddle Monster

The Puddle Monster is splashy and splooshy.
It leaps out of the puddle, but I vanquish it.

I don't think *splooshy* is a word.

I made up another word! I am an inventor!
I imagine that I am an inventor. With a laboratory
of inventions. Spell distracts me from my inventor
dream.

Spell writes: **One splashy, splooshy Puddle
Monster coming up.**

A mucky, muddy circle of water leaps up from the
puddle. It is HUGE! Much bigger than I imagined.
Bigger than me. I throw myself forward and try to
vanquish it. The puddle screams and splooshes away
down the block!

I write. Spell! I didn't *vanquish* the puddle!
It ran away.

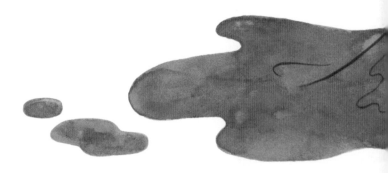

I, um, wasn't sure what *vanquish* means.

It means FIGHT AND WIN!
It means TO DEFEAT!

I notice a little bit
of water on Spell.
Whoops! Luckily,
it's only a few
drops.

I shake the water off Spell and me. Then I put Spell in one of my deep pockets. *Deep* is an adjective. Like *super*. And *stunning*. And *spectacular*. Ms. Hairball calls adjectives *describing words* because they describe things. I love adjectives. I love describing words because I want to be a writer when I grow up. Writers love describing things.

Trixie is my best friend. Her purple house is five houses down my block. Purple is an adjective, too. I try to think of more adjectives for her house: pretty, modern, spandangly. I don't know if *spandangly* is a word. Maybe I made up another word!

I splash through puddles to her pristine front door. *Pristine* means perfect and tidy—Trixie and her mom are both perfectly tidy all the time! I knock our secret-code triple-knock. One loud *KNOCK!* And then two little quick ones—*knock, knock.*

Trixie glides out of her house. She thinks walking like this makes her look like a movie star. She wants to be a movie star more than anything.

"Hurry up, girls," Trixie's mom says.

Together, Trixie and I wade through another gigantic puddle. I check around for the Puddle Monster, but it is gone.

Trixie and I race the one block to school. I win. Before we go in, we wave goodbye to Trixie's mom. Then we join the crowd of kids rushing to get to their classrooms before the late bell.

We arrive at Room 3B as the bell rings. Ms. Hairball has the nicest classroom in the whole school. She has *fairy lights* dangling all over the room, every wall is decorated with poems, and she has a book corner. Ms. Hairball is sitting in her reading chair. She is small and round like an apple. She has a smiley, rosy face. Also like an apple. Best of all, Ms. Hairball is a published author. Not like an apple.

As the kids come in, they sit on the rug in front of the reading chair. The other kids are all squirming. Dawson Dawsons squirms the most. (I *know*, he has a splendid name! I wish my name was Polly Pollys!)

Ms. Hairball is extra shiny today. Her gray dress is sleek, too. *Sleek* is a word my dad uses to describe cabinets.

He is a contractor,
and he knows a lot
of contractor words!
Ms. Hairball is sleek and shiny and smiling.
(Three **S** adjectives. Super!)
    She sits silently. (More **S** words.
This is getting SILLY!)

Finally, 3B settles down. Even Dawson Dawsons.

Ms. Hairball announces, "As you all know, today we are having our school fair."

Everyone starts talking excitedly. Dawson Dawsons jumps and bounces and whoops. Like he has fireworks in his pants. Obviously, he doesn't really have fireworks in his pants. That is a simile.

A *simile* is when you say something is *like* something else. And *simile* is one letter away from the word *smile*. An extra reason for me to love similes.

"One, two, three, eyes on me," Ms. Hairball says. She lifts her fingers one, two, three.

"One, two, eyes on you," we all reply.

"Who can remember the theme of the school fair?" she asks.

Uh, so easy! "It's books!" I call out.

"Remember to raise your hand, Polly. But yes, you're right. Our school fair theme is books. We are partnering with S.T.O.R.Y. Utopia."

Utopia is the name of our town. *Utopia* means perfect place. But Utopia the town is a perfect*ly* ordinary and boring place. S.T.O.R.Y. Utopia helps kids and families read together.

Ms. Hairball continues, "S.T.O.R.Y. Utopia will set up the fair for us. I hope some of you were able to bring a used book to donate to their reading programs."

I put my shiny new dictionary on the pile. "I'm donating my new one, Ms. Hairball. My ancient dictionary is too precious."

"Thank you, Polly. That is very kind."

I beam.

Without putting up his hand, Dawson Dawsons asks, "When can we get popcorn?"

"I'm sorry to disappoint you, class. S.T.O.R.Y. Utopia says their popcorn machine is broken. No popcorn."

We all groan.

"Time for quiet reading and writing, class."

We all go to our desks. I open Spell. I remember how Ms. Hairball told me that I am very kind! I fill up with happiness, like I am a cup filling up with hot tea.

Helping feels good. I am helping by donating a book.

I feel an idea floating in my mind like a shiny bubble. Everyone is going to be SO happy with my help.

THREE

I write in Spell: We can't have a school fair without popcorn. We need to fix this problem. Popcorn PLUS books will be extra delicious. We can call it Pop-Open-A-Book-Corn!

Spell writes back: **Pop-Open-A-Book-Corn —perfect!**

Exactly!

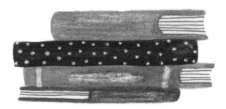

More names for things at the fair:

∧∧∧∧∧∧∧∧∧∧∧∧∧∧∧∧

Title-Tastic-Photo-Booth

Book-Face-Painting

Oooh, I hope they have cotton candy!

But I can't think of a punnier name for it!

Punnier?

A pun is a word-joke.

Get it? *Punnier* instead

of *funnier*!

Very funny! Very

punny! What is cotton

candy, anyway?

It's like fluffy sugar clouds!

Wow! We could call it

Cotton-Cloud-Candy!

Super!

More ideas:

— — — — — — —

A Read-A-Coaster

A Book Odyssey

How about a Book Carousel?

Book-A-Look?

Look! A book!

I giggle.
Ms. Hairball
tells us to
put away our
books. I tuck
Spell into my
cubby very
safely.

Ms. Hairball loves lists. I do, too.

She gives each kid five blank index cards. We all write five book titles, one on each card. Everyone in the school is doing it. It's for the school fair. All the cards will go in a huge jar. Then people can guess how many *different* books are in the jar to win a prize. I bet the prize is a book.

A List of Incredible Books for the Book-Title Jar

Each Kindness

Guinness World Records

Shai & Emmie Star in Dancy Pants

Ruby and the Booker Boys

I can't decide what number five should be:

The Merriam-Webster Dictionary

Or:

Ivy + Bean

I spend so long not deciding that

Ms. Hairball gives me another index card.

I am allowed to write them both!

When we finish our book-jar lists, we do math. We guesstimate the number of words on a page of *The Flat Earth Theory* (by Ms. Hairball!). To figure out the answer, everyone in the class has to count the number of words in one line. Ms. Hairball helps us add up the words. My guess was way too low! A lot of words go into writing a book!

The morning whizzes by. At lunch recess, Trixie talks about a movie she wants to see. Hannah and Luala do handstands.

I practice my handstand next to Luala.

"I bet I can stay upside down longer than you both!" I say.

All the blood rushes to my head. My tummy and legs get wobbly. I tumble over. Hannah tumbles over next.

Luala stays upside down. She doesn't even seem out of breath.

The bell rings. Luala flips right-way-up and we all head toward class. In the hallway, there is a stack of books on a table. Our principal, Mr. Love, picks up a book and opens it. As he opens the pages, out pops lots and lots of popcorn! *Pop. Pop. Pop!*

"It's a Pop-Open-A-Book-Corn stall," I blurt out. "I wrote that in Spell!!!"

"I seeeee," he says. He always makes his words veeery loooong.

Someone from S.T.O.R.Y. Utopia comes over and opens another popping-corn book.

"Oh," she says. "Well. Yum." She eats some popcorn. Then she walks over to a table that has a sign that says BOOK-FACE-PAINTING! Just like what I wrote in Spell!

We try to peek into the library, to see if S.T.O.R.Y. Utopia is setting up the Book Carousel I wrote about in Spell. But the library doors are closed so we can't see.

Back in class, Aarav and I work on tidying up the classroom bookshelves. I love his name because he has TWO **A**s at the start. Although Polly has two **L**s in it, it is not as good a name as Aarav. Even Anna's name is better than mine! Anna's name has two **N**s in the middle AND can be spelled backward and forward. That makes her name a palindrome.

I've asked my mom if I can get a new name. Maybe Ava or Layal or Pip or Neven. All palindromes! But Mom always tells me that my name is special because I am named after Dad's great-great-grandmother. I try to explain that his great-great-grandmother might be double-great, but her name is still not my favorite. Mom doesn't understand. But that's because MOM is *also* a palindrome!

I think about my favorite palindromes. We have finished cleaning up, so I go to get Spell and write:

My Favorite Palindromes:

Wonton? Not now!

A man, a plan, a canal—Panama!

Go, dog!

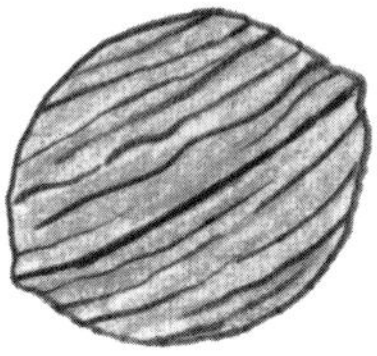

Spell writes:

**A nut for
a jar of tuna.**

I laugh. Then
the final bell
rings. Woo-hoo!
The fair is about
to begin.

FOUR

I rush through the crowd to find my family of Diamonds. Our last name is Diamond, so I always think of my family as sparkling.

The S.T.O.R.Y. Utopia book donation box is by the main doors. The Cotton-Cloud-Candy machine is near the recycling bins. Little clouds of cotton candy puff toward the ceiling. Kids are jumping up to catch them. The Title-Tastic-Photo-Booth is in the hallway that goes to the gym. People are lining up to take photos with props from great books. I spot a broomstick and a witch's hat. Maybe later I'll dress up as Winnie the Witch!

I see my family sparkling like diamonds in the front foyer.

Dad is holding baby Finn. Anna hangs off my Mom's arm like a purse. I hop-skip-jump over to them.

"This is the awesomest," I say.

I love how adding the letters **est** make a word mean more.

"Wildest, wackiest, weirdest," my dad replies. Like me, he loves words.

Baby Finn yells.

"Hey there, little Finn Basil," I say, rubbing his tiny arm. He gives me a gummy smile. I ask my family, "Can you all come see my poster? Everyone in the class made one."

As we walk down the hallway, Anna begs for cotton candy. She begs for popcorn. She begs for face-painting.

Mom says, "We're going to look at Polly's poster first."

"But Mo-o-om," Anna says. For a three-and-a-half-year-old, she has a scary-good whine.

"Oh, Polly," Mom says, when she sees my poster. "You worked so hard on this. Well done. Lovely handwriting."

Reading Rules

By Polly Diamond

A Book Is Like a Milkshake: If you don't like one flavor, try a different one.

A Book Is Like a Piece of Toast: Some days, you want to eat toast. Some days, you do not want toast. Some days, you want to eat two or three pieces of toast!

Some Books Are Like Cakes: It takes ages for cakes to bake. Sometimes it takes ages to read a book. But then it's really good!

A Book Is Like a Meal: It fills you up. But then later you want another one!

For my last rule, I wanted to write *Treat ALL books like they can write back to you.* Like Spell. But Spell is my magic secret. In the end, I put:

Treat books like they are scrumptious and full of magic!

"Super-duper poster, Polly D," Dad says. He is beaming. Ms. Hairball comes over and says, "Polly's poster is excellent work."

"Hi, Lori!" Mom says.

Mom's best friend is named Lori Arbul. (We call her Ms. Hairball!) This means that sometimes Ms. Hairball comes to babysit. This is the best. Other times, Ms. Hairball's niece Shaylene comes to babysit. This is not the best.

A List of Annoying Things About Shaylene

1. She says I read too many books and they will make my eyes go googly.
2. She does not know how to spell *turquoise*.
3. She has green hair. Not turquoise hair.

Wow! Just when I thought about Shaylene, she appeared in Ms. Hairball's classroom. Maybe I have magic powers. I scrunch up my nose and try to make her disappear.

"Hello, Mr. and Mrs. Diamond. Hello, Auntie Lori," Shaylene says.

My magic trick has not worked. Shaylene is still here. Being yucky polite. But she does not say hello to me. Instead, she takes a selfie. Then another.

Mom turns her head. "Where's Anna?" she asks.

"She was right here a minute ago," Dad says.

I spin around. Where *is* Anna?

A lurchy feeling goes through my tummy. Like I'm on Anna's rocking horse. Anna is very annoying. Like Shaylene. But Anna is also little.

And now she is lost in my school. My big, busy, bustling school.

We race out of my classroom.

FIVE

Hannah and Luala are standing by a large sign that hangs over the walkway to the older kids' classrooms. The bubbly letters read: BOOK ODYSSEY. I love the word *Odyssey*—two **Y**s and two **S**s. But only three syllables. OD-ys-sey. The word is from a very old book called *The Odyssey*. *Odyssey* means *journey*. I imagine myself on a journey, perhaps to the moon in a rocket. I circle the moon three times. Then I zoom back to my school walkway to find Anna.

The walkway is filled with lots of large posters.

They are designed like travel ads.

FOR A MAGICAL FAMILY VACATION, VISIT THE LAND OF STORIES!

INVESTIGATE LOND *with* SHERLOCK HOLM

"We're looking for Anna. Have you seen her?"
I ask Hannah and Luala.

They shake their heads.

"What if she is lost forever!" Shaylene cries.

"It's okay, Shaylene, she won't be far," says
Dad. But his eyebrows are frowning and his eyes
are darting left and right.

I think, think, think about my sister.
I search, search, search my brain for the answer,
like I am looking for my turquoise pen. I lose
my turquoise pen so often that Mom says
we should glue it to my hand.

Where would Anna
go? I think about
what she said as
we walked to my
classroom.

Oh, yeah, she was being Queen of the Whiners. She
wanted Pop-Open-A-Book-Corn. And Cotton-Cloud-
Candy. And Book-Face-Painting.

"I think I know where she is," I call over my
shoulder. I'm already running. My family and
Shaylene run after me.

We check the Pop-Open-A-Book-Corn stand.
And the Cotton-Cloud-Candy stall. Then we race to
the Book-Face-Painting booth. Anna is surrounded
by older kids. The tallest Eighth Grader is saying to
her, "You are *so* cute!"

"I know," Anna replies. She takes a huge mouthful of popcorn. "Oh, hi, Mom."

I am so glad to see her! I squeeze her like she is my favorite stuffie.

Mom grabs Anna from me. She hugs her, too. Then she starts a lecture about staying where we can see her.

"I can help look after Anna," Shaylene says.

"Oh, thank you, Shaylene," Mom says. "Maybe you can wait in the face-painting line with her?"

"Of course, Mrs. Diamond."

"I want to be a fairy," Anna says.

I have an idea! Maybe I can help Anna's face-painting be super special for her!

I hurry down the hallway to get Spell from my cubby.

My classroom is quiet and the fairy lights make it feel magical. I've never been alone in here before. It's weird. I tiptoe over and grab Spell.

I write: The character face-painting is the best ever! The paint colors are so bright, we will look just like the pictures in our favorite books. The glitter paint sparkles so much, we will be magical. We will look so . . .

I try to think of a good adjective. One pops into my head.

I write: . . . realistic that our teachers and parents will be super surprised!

Spell writes: **Okay, Polly.**

I carry Spell back with me to the Book-Face-Painting table. An Eighth Grader sits opposite Anna carefully drawing a fairy onto Anna's left cheek. She dabs a final brushstroke.

Then she adds a little silver glitter paint, and—
poof!—the fairy from my sister's cheek zings to life!
It flutters around Anna's head.

The Eighth Grader giggles. "Wow.
This is cool!" She draws more little
fairies, and they all zip and spark
to life and fly around Anna's head.
I didn't expect this! I think
about what I wrote in Spell. Oh!
Spell has made the face-painting
magical and
REAL-istic!
Wow!

Now Anna's face
is being painted with
swirls and sparkles to
make her look like a fairy, too.
She begins to glow. Anna is turning
into a fairy!
A pink-and-silver fairy! With glorious wings!
She reminds me of Carmen the Cheerleading Fairy.
That is Anna's favorite fairy from one of my books!
She always wants to read my books.

At the next table over, Dawson Dawsons is being painted green. He is beginning to glow, too. His green face gets fiercer. The scales painted on his face start to glow. Dawson Dawsons is turning into the green dragon from *How to Train Your Dragon*. The one with TWO HEADS!

Maybe I should call him Dragon Dragons!

He flicks his two dragon tails.

I overhear a parent say, "That dragon is so realistic!"

"Verrrrrrrry realistic," our principal, Mr. Love, replies slowly, like his mouth is pulling the letters from deep in his tummy! "We have Merrrrrrrlin over there. He looks a bit like Mr. Novakoski."

I hear Anna say, "You should get your face painted, Shaylene!"

"Um, I don't know," Shaylene replies.

"You could be Super Diaper Baby," I suggest.

"Ewwww," Shaylene says.

"What about Ulysses from the book *Flora & Ulysses*?"

"What is that?" Shaylene asks. Her eyes narrow.

"Ulysses is very smart," I say. I do not say that Ulysses is also a squirrel.

"Okay. Good idea, Polly."

It's fantastic! The school fair is becoming spectacular!

Ideas pop into my head like popcorn from a Pop-Open-A-Book-Corn book.

I remember the names that Spell and I came up with. I find a quiet spot and start writing. The Book Carousel has characters from *Alice's Adventures in Wonderland* on it. They can move and talk! And the Read-A-Coaster has wagons that we can sit in.

I think about how Luala and Hannah did handstands this morning.

I write: The wagons go upside down, like on a real roller coaster. And the Book Odyssey is a fantastic . . .

I think of some more adjectives.

I write: . . . magical, extraordinary journey.

Spell writes: **A Read-A-Coaster? Great!**

I write back: It is great. And, double-great, Shaylene is going to turn into a squirrel!

I hear someone yell, "A unicorn!" Like the one from the book *Phoebe and Her Unicorn*!

I'm about to go and look when I hear a scratching at my feet. A very angry little squirrel, with a tuft of green hair, natters at me. Shaylene! I look at what I just wrote.

I guess now Shaylene is just a regular squirrel.

Not as smart as Ulysses the squirrel.

She chatters at me and I smile at her. "Let's go and have fun, Shaylene!"

Shaylene sticks her squirrel tongue out at me and runs in the other direction.

SIX

I find Mom, Dad, and Anna in the crowd in the foyer waiting to see the Book Carousel. Shaylene the squirrel runs up to them.

Anna bends down and waves a finger. "Hi, Shaylene!" she says. She really is very smart for a three-and-a-half-year-old. Anna tries to tell Mom that Shaylene is a squirrel. But Mom is shushing baby Finn. I put Spell down and try to help her. Baby Finn yells more. I know he loves me. But right now he's as angry as a tiny bear.

"Don't worry about Finn," Mom says. "You've worked so hard on the fair—go enjoy it with your friends."

I see Luala and Trixie walking together to the schoolyard. I catch up with them outside.

The chatter of excited kids fills the air. Next to Room 5A's vegetable box is a roller coaster. A real roller coaster. I think about what I wrote in Spell. *Just like a real roller coaster!* Its wagons are painted to look like books. And one of the wagons has a turquoise cover. Just like Spell.

Luala, Trixie, and
I wait for the turquoise
wagon to come around. Then the
three of us climb in.

The wagon creaks under our feet.
We strap in. Before I can catch my breath,
we whoosh into the air. *Wheeee!* The roller
coaster loops and swoops over the school.
We're upside down! Then sideways and spinning
in a corkscrew. We go around and then through
the clouds.

We shudder to a halt back at school. Luala
says, "Now *that* was a roller coaster!"

Trixie is laughing, but she looks a little
green. "Let's try something else," she says.

Before I have time to think, Hannah and Trixie have grabbed my hands. "Off to the Book Carousel!"

When we get to the front of the line at the library, I can hardly believe my eyes. Wow! I had imagined that the Book Carousel would just be one of the regular library carousels for books—the round shelves that spin. I thought it would be decorated with all our favorite books. But Spell has made the carousel into an *actual* carousel, like at a carnival, with characters from the book *Alice's Adventures in Wonderland* to ride on.

The White Rabbit, Mad Hatter, and Dormouse already have people on them. I clamber onto the Cheshire Cat. Trixie sits on the Queen of Hearts. She waves to an imaginary audience. Luala gets onto the Mock Turtle. Tinkling music starts as the ride creaks and begins to move. The Cheshire Cat

goes up and down—not so high at first. Then higher, higher. I can almost touch the library ceiling! We glide round and round. The books on the library shelves whiz by. So. Many. Books. I imagine exploding with happiness like a Polly-Diamond-Sparkle firework.

Trixie screams and points. "Polly! What happened to your cat?"

I look down. Whoa. It's dizzying. It's death-defying. It's GONE! I remember that in the book, the Cheshire Cat vanishes. He leaves only his smile. And now *my* Cheshire Cat has vanished. His smile is all that is left to hold me up!

The music speeds up, and so does the carousel.
The smile rises higher, then drops down. I hold my
arms out for balance. We are going so fast now that
I don't dare jump off, but I don't know how long
I can sit on this smile!

With a sudden clang, the ride judders to a stop.
I judder with it.

Trixie jumps off the Queen of Hearts.
"This fair is wild!" she says.

"Come on!" yells Luala. "Let's
try the Book Odyssey next."

SEVEN

The three of us head over to the Book Odyssey.
But all I see is a pile of carpets. Nothing else.
I guess I didn't give Spell anything other than the
word *fantastic*! But the Book Odyssey doesn't seem
fantastic at all. Where is Spell?

Luala shrugs and tells us she's going to find her
mom. Trixie and I look at the carpets.

"Let's go back to the Read-A-Coaster," she says.

"Wait!" I pull out one of the carpets and lay it in
front of us. What if Spell thought that I meant an
odyssey, like a real journey?! I say to Trixie, "What if
it's a magic carpet?"

Trixie giggles. But she gets onto the carpet with me.

"How do magic carpets work?" I ask.

"I think you have to say where you want to go," says Trixie. "Like in the movies."

"Of course!" My brain starts to swirl with ideas for all the places we could go. Terabithia from the book *Bridge to Terabithia*, or the Maldives, which

Guinness World Records says is the world's flattest country!

"Can we go to Hollywood?" Trixie asks.

"It has to be a place from a book," I reply. "I can't think of a Hollywood book right now!"

"How about London?" Trixie asks.

"I know a book. *The London Eye Mystery.* It's super good."

"To London, my good fellow!" Trixie says in what she thinks is a movie-star British accent.

The carpet wriggles and shakes underneath us.
Trixie and I grab hold of each other. The carpet
starts to fly down the hallway, passing the S.T.O.R.Y.
Utopia posters. We're going faster and faster.
The end of the hallway is getting closer and closer.
And then I see it—a tiny door appears in front
of us. It is sooo tiny, a hamster would just fit
through. It makes me think of the tiny
people in the book *The Borrowers*.
The carpet shudders, then races
toward the tiny doorway.
Trixie and I scream.
We're going to crash!

But suddenly, the tiny door opens and we shoot
through it. Somehow there is plenty of space.
Space enough for a giant to go through! Trixie and
I balance on the carpet. We soar through the air.
We are high, high, high in the sky. But even as the
carpet swishes from side to side, we don't fall off.

We both slowly relax
and start to look around.

"Look!" I point below. Through the clouds, I
see green fields. In the distance are thousands of
buildings. Millions. We speed over the rooftops.
A white dome appears. "The Millennium Dome!"
I cry. "Did you know that the world's loudest scream
was recorded at the Millennium Dome? I read about
it in Guinness World Records!"

Trixie screams, just for fun. It is very loud!
Maybe she has just set a new world record!

Like a glittery snake, a river wiggles along below us. The boats look like toys from up here.

"The River Thames! Look at the boats and bridges!" I see a large Ferris wheel. "That's the London Eye," I say. "And there are the Houses of Parliament. Did you know that the world's tallest man and the world's shortest man had tea on Guinness World Records Day right there!" I point at a grassy bank opposite the Houses of Parliament. "I read about it!"

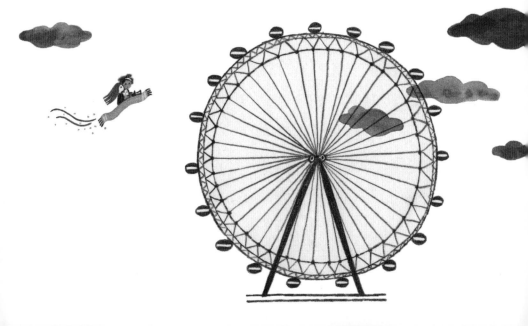

We veer away from the river and glide over a park. Now below us lies a huge white building surrounded by black fences. Teeny black-fuzzy-hatted guards march around.

"It's Buckingham Palace," I call out. "I read about it when I was little—in the book *Paddington at the Palace*! And in *The Royal Rabbits of London*! They live in a warren underneath the palace!"

"Tea with the royal family," Trixie says. She pretends to drink a cup of tea, her pinky raised. "I keep thinking we'll see Mary Poppins flying past us!"

We swoop around one more corner. I remember reading about fancy English tea parties in the book *The Winding Road to London*, by Esmeralda Rock.

The carpet whizzes away from the palace gates and crosses the park. We see a long garden filled with roses leading to a huge house. The windows are the tallest I've ever seen. Inside are chandeliers, a long table, and tapestries.

I notice a small window on the top floor. I know from my word-a-day calendar that this top floor is called a garret. The carpet floats toward the garret window. Inside, a woman sits at a desk. She is typing on a laptop. Beside her are shelves of books.

Many of the books have the same name on them: Esmeralda Rock. The author!

"I've read her books!" I whisper.

Esmeralda glances up. Her eyebrows gather. She squints. She rubs her eyes. Then she comes to the window and waves at us!

The carpet turns. We hurtle through the air. Glimmering in the middle of a cloud is a doorway the size of a box of crayons. Oh, no! Here we go again! Trixie and I scream. The door opens. We whiz through.

We land in our school hallway.

There is a huge roar.

Trixie and I jump off the carpet.

Then there is another roar!

EIGHT

Trixie and I push our way to the front of a crowd, and we see Dragon Dragons and a unicorn racing a shaggy dog. It looks like the dog in the book *Because of Winn-Dixie*. I wonder if it is Hannah. She loves that book.

Dragon Dragons is roaring very loudly. And he is definitely winning. He's half running and half flying. Suddenly, the shaggy dog speeds up. It passes the dragon. It is definitely Hannah. She is the fastest kid in our class. She waves a paw and woofs. The dragon roars.

The clouds of cotton candy have grown bigger. Now they fill the ceilings and gloop down the walls. That is a lot of cotton candy!

Two teachers hustle past. They are chasing the Big Bad Wolf. Tweedledum and Tweedledee have escaped the carousel. They bustle toward the race.

Dragon Dragons roars at them.

The wolf runs after Little Red Riding Hood.

Mr. Love yells, "Slooooooow doooooown!"

Ms. Hairball is flapping her arms around. She looks like she has been in a hot oven. Her face is sweaty and red. Her hair is sticking up. She looks a bit like she is losing her mind. I imagine her mind like a hamster scurrying around the school.

Someone screams from the carousel. I bet they are balancing on the smile.

Shaylene the squirrel races through the hallway.
She scrambles onto the Book-Title Jar.

"A rodent!" yells Trixie's mom.

Someone's dad starts trying to thwack Shaylene
with a broomstick—the prop from the photo
booth.

I do not like Shaylene. But I do not
want her thwacked by a broom.

Shaylene skirts the broomstick
and races outside.

Phew!

Mr. Love yells,
"Marvellloooous fair,
but it's time to
wrap up!"

No one
listens.

Except me. I think Mr. Love is right. It is time
to write in Spell. Spell will help wrap up this fair
quickly. I giggle. If I wrote Wrap up the school
fair in Spell, Spell would probably wrap us all up in
wrapping paper. But, where is Spell?

I look in the roller coaster. Spell is not there.
I look around the rest of the playground. I don't see
Spell anywhere. Oh, no. I think I have lost Spell.

I do lose things a lot.

Things I Have Lost

My glasses—lots
My turquoise pen—lots
My dinosaur backpack
The invitation to Hannah's party
My sister!

A worried feeling goes through me like a slippery eel. *Eel* is a great word. I also like the word *aardvark*. When I lose things, my mom tells me to retrace my steps. She says: *Concentrate, Polly. Think about where you have been.* Just like I did when we lost Anna.

My dad usually adds, *Concentrate means get your head straight!* Then he usually puts his thumbs in his ears and waggles his hands and his whole head— like his head might fall off!

I go to my classroom. I check my cubby. I check my desk. I check my jacket pocket. No Spell. I check them all again.

An icky-sticky thought churns in my tummy. Then I remember:

The donation box!

What if someone found Spell? And put Spell in the donation box by mistake?

I run to the front foyer. The White Witch chats with Little Red Riding Hood. Next to a big, empty space. The donation box is gone.

"Excuse me," I ask Little Red Riding Hood. "Where is the box of donation books?"

"Mrs. Akl and Ms. Arbul took the books to Ms. Arbul's car. Oh, I'd better go. The wolf is coming." She tugs her hood up and rushes off.

I rush to the parking lot. I see a lot of muddy puddles. But I do not see Mrs. Akl or Ms. Hairball.

Spell is gone. I have lost my magic book.

NINE

Tears fill my eyes. They slide behind my glasses. They drip down my cheeks.

Spell is the best book I've ever had.

I love novels and poems and true stories and dictionaries.

But in Spell, I can write anything. With my book, I can go anywhere. I can be anyone. Now Spell is lost. Donated.

Shaylene the squirrel is in the tree by the parking lot. She throws a nut at me.

"Hey, Shaylene," I call up to her. "I'm sorry, but I can't turn you back into a person."

I guess Shaylene being a squirrel is not so bad. At least she can't take selfies!

She clambers down the tree. She holds her little squirrel hands out, as if she's asking me what I'm talking about.

"I lost my magic book. It has gone with Ms. Hairball to be donated."

Shaylene shakes her squirrel head. She runs away, then runs back. She wants me to follow her. I run after her. She turns the corner of the school. There is another small parking lot there. And right in the middle: Ms. Hairball's car. Her trunk is open. It is full of books.

Ms. Hairball is standing to one side of her car, deep in conversation with Merlin. Who I think is Mr. Novakoski.

Shaylene jumps onto the hood of the car. She natters at me again, this time pointing at the books. I start to riffle through the donated books.

A noise from the other side of the car makes me turn. It is a splashy, splooshy noise.

The Puddle Monster! It is mucky and muddy and huge. It drips around the car.

"Stay away from the books!" I cry.

The Puddle Monster wibbles and wobbles.

"Don't get them wet!"

The Puddle Monster gets closer. It drips on my arm.

"Okay, you!" I cry. "You asked for it." I swipe my shiny dictionary from the pile. I swoosh it around my head.

"I will vanquish you!"

The Puddle Monster screams and runs away. Shaylene claps her little squirrel hands.

I keep searching through the books.

Ms. Hairball and Mr. Wizard-Novakoski notice us. "Is everything okay, Polly?"

"I have lost my magic book," I say.

Ms. Hairball shakes her head. "Your turquoise writing book? It isn't in here. I would have noticed it."

My heart sinks. I feel it drop down into my tummy like a stone through water. I sigh. I look once more at the donated books. Ms. Hairball is right. Spell is not in the trunk. Spell is not in the donation pile.

Shaylene the squirrel chatters at me. I bet she is saying, "What if Spell is lost forever!" Just like she said about Anna when Anna was lost.

Anna! I remember when we were looking for Anna earlier. Then we found her. Then I wrote about character face-painting in Spell. Then I came back to find my family. And now I remember!

I left Spell on the low wall in the foyer.

"Come with me, Shaylene!" I say to Shaylene the squirrel.

Ms. Hairball looks puzzled. But I am running too fast to care. Shaylene rushes along with me. We dash to the foyer. I look on the low wall. Spell is not there. My heart starts to sink again. But then I spot my family.

I see that Anna the fairy is holding something turquoise. She is cuddling it like it's a doll.

"My book!" I yell.

Anna says, "You lost it.
I found it. Like you found me."
She really, really, really is very
smart for a three-and-
a-half-year-old.

I grab Spell. "Thank
you, you super stunning spectacular sister!"
I squeeze, squeeze, squeeze her.

Then, I open up Spell. Spell writes: **Mr. Owl ate my metal worm!**

What?

It's a palindrome. Do you like it?

I love it! I'm so glad I found you.

Dragon Dragons comes running into the foyer.
He belches, and a small puff of flame comes from
one of his mouths. Oh, no. He's figured out how to
blow fire!

Quickly, I write in Spell: Dawson Dawsons is a boy.

With a flash, Dawson appears instead of the two-headed dragon. Next to him appears another identical Dawson.

I write: No, Spell! That's his name. He is only one boy. His name is Dawson Dawsons!

What a great name!

I know! But can you make him one boy? Two Dawsons is too many!

There is another flash, and Dawson Dawsons is back to his usual self. Except when he walks away, he swishes his butt as if he still had a tail. I write: Spell, we have to clean up. First, we need to put the carousel away. Then we should pack up the Cotton-Cloud-Candy stall.

A huge creaking sound comes from the library— and then a smash and a boom from near the gym.

I run to the gym and see that Spell has stuffed the carousel into the equipment room. The Cheshire Cat yowls from underneath the gym mats. Eeek! Lining one side of the gym are several boxes. I open one nervously. It is full of sticky cotton candy.

I write: Spell, we need to tidy up!

There is a rumble and a whoosh. The boxes start to float into the air.

I write: NO! Not up in the air. Okay. Wait.

I think about how to get the right words into my book. Perhaps I should write a story. I am a very good writer!

A Story About the End of the School Fair

The stalls are finished. The rides are all done. The fair is over. Everyone is themselves. They loved being characters from books. Everyone has had a great day. The kids are happy, the adults are smiling, the teachers are delighted. The school is clean, tidy, and ready for school next week.

Sounds perfect.

Sounds super, stunning, and spectacular.

Trixie, Luala, and Hannah wave goodbye.

Dawson Dawsons roars a goodbye, even though he is no longer a real dragon.

I carry Spell over to my family. Baby Finn sleeps against my mom. When he is asleep, he looks cute. Cute for a squished-up baby, anyway.

Mom says, "What
an outstanding fair."

Outstanding has to be one of the best
words ever. Outstanding. Standing Out.

"Polly, can I be a fairy again?" Anna asks.

"Sure," I whisper. She is very smart for a three-and-
a-half-year-old. Much smarter than the grown-ups.
"But not now. Now it's time to go home."

I hug Spell close to me as we walk outside.

"Help! Mr. and Mrs. Diamond! Help! Polly!" Shaylene shouts. She is up a tree, but she is not a squirrel anymore. Below her, the Puddle Monster splooshes and splashes.

"Shaylene needs wings," Anna says.

I giggle. "That is a super stunning spectacular idea, Anna!"

I open Spell. And begin to write.

The End.

POLLY'S FAVORITE BOOKS!

(How many have you read?)

‎〜〜〜〜〜〜〜〜〜

Each Kindness by Jacqueline Woodson

Guinness World Records (any year!)

Shai & Emmie Star in Dancy Pants!
by Quvenzhané Wallis

Ruby and the Booker Boys by Derrick Barnes

The Merriam-Webster Dictionary

Ivy + Bean by Annie Barrows

The Flat Earth Theory by Lori Arbul*

Winnie the Witch by Valerie Thomas

Carmen the Cheerleading Fairy by Daisy Meadows

How to Train Your Dragon by Cressida Cowell

The Adventures of Super Diaper Baby by Dav Pilkey

Flora & Ulysses by Kate DiCamillo

Alice's Adventures in Wonderland by Lewis Carroll

Phoebe and Her Unicorn by Dana Simpson

Bridge to Terabithia by Katherine Paterson

The Borrowers by Mary Norton

Paddington at The Palace by Michael Bond

The Royal Rabbits of London by Santa
Montefiore and Simon Sebag Montefiore

Mary Poppins by P. L. Travers

The Winding Road to London by Esmeralda Black*

Because of Winn-Dixie by Kate DiCamillo

*You can't read *The Flat Earth Theory* or *The Winding
Road to London* because those books aren't real!

ALICE KUIPERS is the author of eight books for young
adults and children. Her books have been published in 34 countries
and have won lots of awards. Born in London, she now lives in Canada
with her partner, the author Yann Martel, their four children, and their
dog, Bamboo. Alice has writing tips and ideas for any budding writers
on her website, including a free course for young writers. Come and
find her there: www.alicekuipers.com.

DIANA TOLEDANO'S name is pronounced "Deanna"
because she is from Spain. Like Polly, she has curly hair and wears
glasses. She grew up in Madrid where she studied art and art history.
In addition to working as an illustrator, she also teaches workshops.
She lives in San Francisco, where she shares a hundred-year-old house
with her husband, a fluffy cat, and a crazy kitten. Learn more about
her at www.diana-toledano.com.